# It's a Bird!

Elisa Peters

**PowerKiDS** press™

New York

*For Jackie Patton*

Published in 2009 by The Rosen Publishing Group, Inc.
29 East 21st Street, New York, NY 10010

First Edition

Editor: Amelie von Zumbusch
Book Design: Greg Tucker
Photo Researcher: Jessica Gerweck

Photo Credits: All images by Shutterstock.com.

Library of Congress Cataloging-in-Publication Data

Peters, Elisa.
  It's a bird! / Elisa Peters. — 1st ed.
      p. cm. — (Everyday wonders)
  Includes index.
  ISBN 978-1-4042-4461-0 (library binding)
  1. Birds—Juvenile literature. I. Title. II. Series.

  QL676.2.P46 2009
  598—dc22

                                                2007046334

Manufactured in the United States of America

# Contents

Birds are covered in **feathers**.

5

Every bird has two wings
and a **beak**.

7

Birds come in many different shapes, sizes, and colors.

Some birds, like this **rainbow lorikeet**, are very colorful.

Many birds eat seeds.

13

Other birds eat berries.

Seabirds, like this **puffin**, most often eat fish.

Mother birds lay eggs in a nest.

In time, baby birds break out of these eggs.

Mother birds take good
care of their babies.

# Words to Know

beak

feathers

puffin

rainbow lorikeet

# Index

**B**
berries, 14

**E**
eggs, 18, 20

**F**
fish, 16

**S**
seeds, 12

# Web Sites

Due to the changing nature of Internet links, PowerKids Press has developed an online list of Web sites related to the subject of this book. This site is updated regularly. Please use this link to access the list:
www.powerkidslinks.com/wonder/bird/